Grant Stevenson

Pot pourri of gifts literary and artistic

Contributed as a souvenir of the Grand Masonic bazaar

Grant Stevenson

Pot pourri of gifts literary and artistic
Contributed as a souvenir of the Grand Masonic bazaar

ISBN/EAN: 9783337221676

Printed in Europe, USA, Canada, Australia, Japan

Cover: Foto ©Andreas Hilbeck / pixelio.de

More available books at **www.hansebooks.com**

Pot Pourri

The Crown of St. Giles.

Pot Pourri

of

Gifts Literary and Artistic

CONTRIBUTED AS A SOUVENIR OF THE GRAND MASONIC BAZAAR
IN AID OF THE ANNUITY FUND OF SCOTTISH MASONIC
BENEVOLENCE, EDINBURGH 1890

EDITED BY

W. GRANT STEVENSON, A.R.S.A.

R.W.M. OF LODGE DRAMATIC AND ARTS, No. 757

PRINTED FOR LODGE DRAMATIC AND ARTS, No. 757,
BY TURNBULL & SPEARS, THISTLE STREET,
EDINBURGH   1890

Preface

THE *LODGE DRAMATIC AND ARTS*, No. 757, begs most gratefully to thank those Authors and Artists who have so generously devoted their literary and artistic gifts to the production of this interesting Souvenir of the Grand Masonic Bazaar. Contributions have been received from those outside the Craft,—but charity claims us all in a common brotherhood ; and it will doubtless be a source of pleasure to all who have contributed their offerings, that the Annuity Fund of Scottish Masonic Benevolence will be substantially benefited by their efforts.

December 1890.

Contents

List of Illustrations

A

Pot Pourri

MEG lifting the lid of the Pot, an odour was diffused through the place, which, if the vapours of a witch's cauldron could in aught be trusted, promised something better than the hell-broth which such vessels are usually supposed to contain. It was, in fact, the savour of a goodly stew, composed of fowls, hares, partridges and moor game, boiled in a large mess with vegetables and sweet herbs, and from the look of the cauldron, appeared to be prepared for a multitude of people.

"Hae, then," said she, heaving a portion of the mess into a cream-coloured dish and strewing it savourily with salt and pepper, "there's what will warm your heart."

"I do not hunger!—*conjuro te!*—that is, I thank you heartily, Mrs Merrilees," stammered the Dominie; for he said to himself, "The savour is sweet; but it hath been cooked in the **Lodge Dramatic and Arts.** Who knoweth what mystic passes have been made over the pot; or with what forbidden rites the ingredients thereof have been gathered together; or what evil purposes they are to serve."

"Awa' wi' ye, ye worricow!" said the sibyl, impatiently noting his hesitation. "Kent ye ever ill ware wi' sae halesome a reek? If ye dinna eat instantly, and put some saul in ye, by the bread and the salt, I'll put it down your throat wi' the cutty spoon. Gape, sinner, and swallow."

Sampson, afraid of eye of newt, and toe of frog, tigers' chauldrons, and so forth, had determined not to venture; but the smell of the stew was fast melting his obstinacy. Hunger and Curiosity are excellent casuists.

"Saul," said Hunger, "feasted with the Witch of Endor." "And," quoth Curiosity, "the salt which she sprinkled upon the food shewed plainly it is not a necromantic banquet, in which that savouring never occurs." "And besides," said Hunger, after the first spoonful, "it is savoury and refreshing viands."

"Eat your fill," said the hostess; "but an ye kenned how the meat was gotten, ye maybe wadna like it sae weel." Sampson's spoon fell, in the act of conveying its load to his mouth. "I hae them that will baith write and read and ride and rin for me," continued Meg. "There's been mony a midnight watch to bring a' that trade together."

"Is that all," thought Sampson, resuming his spoon, and shovelling away manfully. "I will not lack my food upon that argument."

"Now ye maun tak' a dram."

" I will," quoth Sampson. And when he had put this copestone upon Meg's good cheer, he felt, as he said, "mightily elevated and afraid of no evil that could befall him."
—" *Guy Mannering," adapted.*

. . . . . .

The first thing that took captive and subdued Sancho's desire was a Pot, which was never made of the mould of common pots, and around which were men and women cooks, all cunning, all zealous, and all content. So without being able to suffer longer, and having no power for aught else, he came to one of the busy cooks, and with courteous and hungry arguments, entreated that he would let him dip a crust of bread in it.

To which the Cook replied, " Brother, this is not a day over which hunger rules, thanks to the givers of the feast ; alight, and look about thee for a ladle, and skim out a pullet or two, and much good may they do thee."

" I cannot see one," said Sancho.

" Hold on," cried the Cook. " Body o' me ! But what a dainty do-nothing art thou !" Saying this, he took a kettle, and, after a prefatory flourish, plunging it into the pot, he drew out three fat pullets and two wild fowl, and said to Sancho, " Eat, friend, and break thy fast with these skimmings while dinner time is coming."

" I have nothing to put it in," said Sancho.

" Well take it all," said the Cook, " spoon and everything ; for liberal hearts supply all."

" Brother," said the squire, " to this House I hold me. And methinks there can be no better Symbol of Brotherhood than this feasting, where what is given is given with good will, and accepted with thankful heart, and consumed with lusty appetite. Aught else is idle words, for which they will demand an account from us in the next world." Saying this he began anew to assault the contents of the Pot with such sturdy stomach that it awaked that of Don Quixote.

—"*Don Quixote*," *slightly altered.*

Age

PAINT me no lies! full surely I draw breath
    Ten years beyond the proper time to die;
And if you hail me still not far from death,
Your words are traitor to the truth—you lie.
Autumn hath fruits unknown to merry May,
But May hath bloom, and pledge of fruitage too,
And the delight of growing day by day
More strong in substance and more bright in hue.
Age may not grow; if in my span of time
God gave me grace with stretch of pious pains,
From pleasant thoughts to weave a tuneful rhyme,
Or preach a needful truth from well-schooled brains,
Enough: I stirred the soil and plucked the weed,
Where happier hands may cast the fruitful seed.

The Prince's Quest

NCE upon a time, in a far-off country, there lived a Prince who ought to have been very happy but wasn't. He reigned in a gorgeous palace, and was rich, and powerful, and great, and had everything he wanted—that is, at least, he had everything he wanted, except the one thing that he wanted more than anything else on earth, and to obtain which he would have given half his kingdom. He would have given the whole for the matter of that, only he had already promised the other half to any one who would tell him what it was he wanted.

Everybody had a guess at it, but nobody seemed able to hit upon it. Everything that was suggested he had ; everything that wealth could buy, or skill procure, was his already. So at last he appealed to the wise men of the city, and they put their heads together, and found out the wrong thing, and the Prince became more despondent than ever.

In the palace his jovial companions made laugh and jest, and kept the walls for ever echoing to the tune of their noi y merriment.　All day long they hunted the deer through the forest glades, or rode a-hawking in gay cavalcade; and at night there were feasting, and dancing, and song, and the wine ran free, and the mirth ran high, and happiness beamed on every face except the Prince's.　In the midst of all the revelry he sat silent and apart, or shunned the chase to muse alone on what this thing could be, the want of which, with all his wealth, made life seem so unfinished.

"Oh, is there no one who can tell me what I want?" sighed the Prince aloud, one day, as he threw himself down on the ground beside a fallen tree.

"I can."

It was a little old man that spoke; a little bent, withered old man, with wrinkled face and snow-white hair; but his eyes were brighter than a boy's, and his voice was as clear as a sweet-toned bell, and, as he looked down at the Prince from his seat on the tree, he laughed a merry, childish laugh.

The Prince looked up at him, and wondered how he got there, but was too surprised to speak, and only stared in silence at the merry, twinkling eyes.

"Well," said the little old fellow after a while, "shall I tell you?　Would you like to know what it is you want, or have you come to the sensible conclusion that after all it is not worth the knowing?　I think you had better not know," he went on, changing from gay to grave.　"It may make you only more unhappy.　It will bring you pain and trouble. You are young and weak—why seek to know?　Rest with the happiness you have, child.　Joy is only reached through sorrow."

But the Prince heeded not the warning.　All eagerness

and hope, he started up, and caught the old man by the hand, and would not let him go.

"Tell me, you who are wise, and who know," cried he; "tell me and I will seek for it through fire and water. I am strong, not weak—strong to dare, to suffer, and to win. I will find it, if it take me all my life, and cost me all my treasure."

The old man gently laid his hand upon the Prince's head, and a look of pity was in the bright, quick eyes.

"Lad," said he, and his voice was grave and tender, "you shall seek your wish. You shall toil for it, and your brain shall ache. You shall wait for it, and your heart shall pant. You shall pass through sorrow and through suffering on your search; but when you are weary and footsore the thought of it shall strengthen you, when your heart is heaviest the hope of it shall raise you up, and in your darkest hour it shall come to you as the touch of a mighty hand. Prince, it is Love you lack. Go seek it."

So the scales fell from the Prince's eyes, and he stood as one that has suddenly emerged from darkness into light, half-bewildered before he understood. Then stretching out his arms, he called to Love, as though he would draw her down from heaven, and clasp her to his heart.

"Oh, Love," he cried, "why have I been so blind as not to know your messenger, who spoke within me? I might have wandered lonely all my life, uncaring and uncared for, and never dreamed of your dear presence, nor ever have known that it was for need of your sweet voice that all the world seemed drear."

Full of gratitude, he turned to thank his mysterious guide, but the little old man was gone.

The Prince's own sentinels scarcely knew their lord when he returned to the palace, and even the old hall-porter who, twenty years ago, had rocked him on his knee, looked hard at him, and seemed inclined to challenge his breathless entrance. Never was a man so changed in half-an-hour before. Out into the woods had gone a moody, sorrowful youth, with wavering steps and dreamy, downcast eyes, while back had come a gallant Prince, with quick, firm tread, and head thrown back, and eyes that flashed with high resolve. Small wonder if the porter was in doubt.

In the banquet-hall his guests already waited his arrival, and hurrying thither straight, without a word he passed up the crowded room until he reached the daïs at the end, and there he turned and spoke :

" Friends," said the Prince, "rejoice with me, for to-day I have learnt the thing that I want. To-day I have found out what is the only thing on earth that can make me happy —the only thing on earth I have not got—the only thing I cannot do without, and that I mean to seek for till I have found. Let all my true friends join me, and at to-morrow's dawn we will start to search the world for Love."

Then one and all cheered loud and long, and swore that each was his loyal friend, and swore that they would follow him throughout the whole wide world, and they drank a bumper to success, and another one to Love, and never in that palace had a banquet been so gay, and never before had such merry guests feasted in that hall. Long into the night they drank and sang, and their loud laughter filled the palace full, and overflowed through open door and window out into the stillness, and the red deer browsing heard it, and scudded away down the moonlit glens, nor dreamt then of the time when they would fearlessly crop the grass round the very walls of the palace, and rest secure and undisturbed upon its weed-grown terraces.

But no shadow of the coming gloom marred the glittering pageantry on which the morning sun threw down his glory, as gay with silk, and flashing steel, and fluttering plumes, and prancing steeds the gallant train of knights and squires rode slowly down the hill. And hearts were light and hopes were high, but no heart so light as the Prince's, no hopes so high as his, as he rode at the head of that gay throng, the gayest of them all.

At each place that they came to the Prince enquired for Love, but found, to his astonishment, that, though people talked about her a good deal, hardly anyone knew her. Few spoke of her as a reality. Most folks looked upon her as a joke; others, as a popular delusion; while the one or two who owned to having known her seemed half ashamed of the acquaintanceship. There were shams and imitations in abundance, but the real thing, when acknowledged, was considered vulgar, and no one knew or cared what had become of her.

The first place at which they halted was the town of Common-Sense—a most uncomfortable place, all full of close and narrow streets that led to nowhere, and inhabited by a race celebrated for the strength of their lungs, it being reckoned that one man of Common-Sense was equal to a dozen poll-parrots, and could talk down fifty men of Intelligence (their natural enemies) in less than half an hour. The religion of this charming people was touching in its simplicity.

It consisted of a firm and earnest belief that they were infallible, and that everybody else was a fool; and each man worshipped himself.

They were quite indignant when the Prince asked them where Love was.

"We know nothing at all about her," said the men of Common-Sense. "What have we to do with Love? What do you take us for?"

The Prince was too polite to tell them what he took them for, so merely bidding them adieu with a pitying smile, rode off to seek elsewhere for Love.

But he had no better luck at the next place they came to. This was Tom Tiddler's Land, and the people there were very busy indeed. So busy were they, picking up the gold and the silver, that they had not time even to make themselves respectable, and their hands were especially dirty—but then it was rather dirty work.

"Love!" said the people of Tom Tiddler's Land. "We don't keep it. Never heard of it. Don't know what it is. But dare say we could get it for you. What are you willing to go to for it?"

"You can't buy it," explained the Prince. "It is given."

"Then you won't get it here, young man," was the curt reply; and they went on with their grovelling.

At last the Prince came to the City of Science, where he was most hospitably received, and where for the first time he learnt the great truth that everything is just precisely what one always thought it wasn't, and that nothing is what one thinks it is. The inhabitants were all philosophers, and their occupation consisted of finding out things that nobody wanted to know, and in each day proving that what they themselves had stated the day before was all wrong. They were very clever people, and knew everything—Love included. She was there, in the city, they told the delighted Prince, and they would take him to her.

So, after showing him over the town and explaining to him what everything wasn't, they took him into their museum, which was full of the most wonderful things, and in the centre was Love—the most wonderful of them all. The Prince couldn't help laughing when he saw it, but the philosophers were very proud of it. It sat upright and stiff on a straight-backed chair, and was as cold as ice.

"Made it ourselves," said the philosophers. "Isn't it beautiful! Acts by clockwork, and never goes wrong. Warranted perfect in every respect."

"It's very charming," answered the Prince, trying to swallow down his disappointment; "but I'm afraid it's not the sort of thing I wanted."

"Why, what's amiss with it? It's got all the latest improvements."

"Yes," replied the Prince with a sigh, "that's just it; I wanted it with all the old faults."

Again the Prince journeyed on, and came to a town where lived a very knowing people called "Men of the World," who had the reputation of "knowing their way about"—a reputation, the acquirement of which it was difficult to understand, seeing they never, by any chance, went outside their own town—a remarkably small one, although the inhabitants firmly believed that it was the biggest and most important place on earth, and that no other city was worth living in for a day.

A dim oil-lamp burnt night and day in the centre of the town, and the inhabitants were under the impression that all light came from that, for as they crawled about on their hands and knees, and never raised their eyes from the ground, they knew nothing about the sun. When they had crawled once forwards and backwards across their little town, they thought they had seen "life," and would squat in a corner, and yawn, till they died.

When the Prince mentioned the name of Love to these creatures, they burst into a coarse, loud laugh. "Is that what you call it?" said they. "Why, wherever do you come from? We know what you mean, though. Come along." And they took him into a dingy room, and showed him a hideous, painted thing that made him sick to look upon.

"Let us leave this place quickly," said the Prince, turning to his followers. "I cannot breathe in this foul air. Let us get out into God's light again." So they mounted in haste and rode away, leaving the men who "knew their way about" crawling about the ways they knew so well.

Farther and farther into the weary world wandered the Prince on his search; but Love was still no nearer, and though his heart was ever brave, it beat less hopefully every day. Time after time he heard of her, and started off, only to find some worthless sham—a golden image—a dressed-up doll—a lifeless statue—a giggling fool. Shams wherever he went, and men and women worshipping, and hugging them close to their breasts, knowing all the while that they were shams; and each time the Prince turned away, more sick at heart than ever.

And now, not a single one of all who had shouted their

loyalty so loudly was left, when weary, baffled, and dis-
heartened, the Prince at last turned back. A great longing
was upon him to be once more among his own people, and
to see his own land again; and so, with this last hope, he
still toiled on, and each day pressed on quicker, fearing lest
death might overtake him by the way, and that his tired eyes
never more would rest upon the old grey towers and sweet
green woods of home.

But the dreary road came to an end at length, and one
evening he looked down upon his palace, as it lay before him
bathed in the red of the sinking sun. Restful, now, he stood
for a while, feasting his hungry eyes upon the longed-for
sight, and then his thoughts ebbed slowly back to that morning, long ago, when he had bidden it adieu, and had ridden
forth into the world upon his quest for Love.

How changed the place! How changed himself since
then!

He had left it as a gallant Prince with all the pride of
pomp around him, and a gaudy throng of flattering courtiers
at his side. He crept back, broken-hearted and alone. He
had left it standing fair and stately in the morning light, and
bright with life and sound; now it was ruined, desolate, and
silent; the bats flew out of the banquet-hall, and the grass
grew on the hearths. Another had usurped his throne; his
people had forgotten him, and not even a dog was there to
give him a welcome home.

As he passed through the damp, chill rooms a thousand
echoing footsteps started up on every side, as though his
entrance had disturbed some ghostly revel, and when, having
reached a little room that in old times he had been wont to

go to for solitude, he entered, and shut himself in, it seemed as though the frightened spirits had hurried away, slamming a thousand doors behind them.

There, in the darkness, he sat himself down, and buried his face in his hands, and wept; and sat there long through the silent hours, lost in his own bitter thoughts. So lost, that he did not hear a gentle tapping at the door—did not hear the door open, and a timid voice asking to come in—did not hear a light step close beside him, nor see a little maiden sit herself down at his feet—did not know she was there till, at last, with a sigh, he raised his head and looked into the gloom. Then his eyes met hers, and he started, and looked down at the sweet, shy face, amazed, and half in doubt.

"Why, you are Love!" said the Prince, taking her little hands in his. "Where have you been, sweet? I've sought you everywhere."

"Not everywhere," said Love, nestling against him with a little half-sad laugh; "not everywhere. I've been here all the time. I was here when you went away, and I've been waiting for you to come back—so long."

And so the Prince's quest was ended.

JEROME K. JEROME.

Anni Fugaces

ALAS! alas! my fellow feres,
    We may no more deny
The pressure of the speeding years;
    Oor days are driving by.

Already on the downward track
    The posting furies fare;
For virtuous life they will not slack,
    For purpose will not spare.

This is the ill beneath the sun
    That vexes aging men;
Our lease of life is half-gate run
    Before of lease we ken.

We waste, or wair oor strength of youth
    On idols of the ee,
Infidel of the wholesome truth
    Of our mortality.

Ye callants, what avails the strife
    That twyns ye o' your prime?
The dearest gift of life is life,
    The dearest enemy time.

O ne'er can rank or wealth enhance
  The gift that ne'er was awn,
The lovely gift, the glorious chance,
  Ance offer'd, sune withdrawn!

To them wha on the shaded slope
  Are faring doun, like me,
With ever daily dwining hope,
  How fair it taks the ee!

What had been oors from hour of birth
  We learn to value then;
Sweet grow the common joys of earth,
  And dear the face of men.

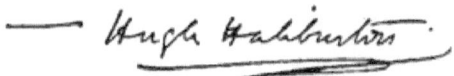
Hugh Haliburton.

Glentirlie

" I HAVE secured quarters at Glentirlie, Charlie; it looks the very place we want. Any number of burns to fish, of hills to climb, braes, glens, and nooks for a botanico-geologist like you to explore or plunder; five miles from a railway station, quite out of the world, and altogether *the* place for us; so get your knapsack and tackle ready for Saturday."

" I will, Frank, I will. Our vacations for some years back have been all we could wish—for the Continent—scenes of beauty, grandeur, or historical interest, brightened by charming fellow-travellers. But I have missed the hills and heather, the banks and braes of our native land. Oh! for a fortnight's browsing in a quiet Scottish valley, to blow away the cobwebs of this year's spinning, and brace us for the next stage."

" Ditto, ditto, Charlie. We have earned a holiday; both of us can say, in cannie mother-country phrase, we have done 'not badly.' True, there have been hard nuts to crack, and middling heavy calls on time and brain, but we have made something out of these, and need a rest: let us resolve to have a thorough one in Glentirlie."

" Spoken like an oracle, Frank. No man will ever appreciate or enjoy a holiday who has not done his level best to deserve it. A fellow that shirks his duty, or does it in a dilly-dallying way has no "spring" in him when on furlough. He is always yawning or lounging; finds this place slow, that 'dead and alive'; runs down what he cannot appreciate, growls at everything and nothing, cannot see what any fellow finds in fishing or climbing, is a bore to others because he is bored by himself. Give such fellows a wide berth. Change of scene and association makes up for the waste of the past, and lays in useful store for the future. Let us rough it in Glentirlie like ancient Britons, coming as near the Aborigines as possible."

"So I shall, Charlie. I shall have a tweed suit for Sundays, for I do like a country kirk with its simple service; but on other days I shall ignore all 'meritricious graces,' collars, cuffs, gloves, razors, and other products of civilisation. My 'rig' will be the motley one in which I do my home-dabbling in photography. It betrays its occupation. No Jewish 'Old Clo'' would soil his bag with it."

"I will follow suit, Frank. My botanico-geological garments have seen many years' service. They were originally roomy and grey, but are now weather-stained enough to grace a museum. Great in pockets, begrimmed outside and in, and shapeless through long service in carrying specimens of all kinds, but of marvellously elastic capacity. Small in buttons as far as numbers go, but rich in variety of shape and metal, and with at least half of the holes (holes most emphatically) marrowless. The hat never was artistic, but, from having been made useful in a variety of ways, it would take a first prize in an exhibition of gipsy head-gear. All need the fresh

air as much as I do, and I will be a " bogle " for six days out
of the seven."

Frank Raeburn and Charles Baillie, whose " crack " we have
recorded, were as fine young fellows as man could wish to
meet. They differed in temperament, for Frank was a bit of
a rattle, and Charlie quieter, but both had the genuine ring
of noble metal. They had been fast friends during and since
their college days, were rising, almost risen young men,
shrewd, painstaking, honourable, and self-respecting ; and
although somewhat under thirty years of age, they were
sought after professionally, and trusted. There was in them
a fine balance of heart, head, and conscience—alike active,
honest, and sterling.

Saturday found the two at the railway station, their knap-
sacks filled with a quaint assortment of old attire, much of
which had been long neglected in odd corners. Their spirits
rose as they left Edinburgh behind them, and were high as
they alighted at the little station of Clearburn. There, mine
host of Glentirlie awaited them ; and his trusty, if rather
clumsy " Dawtie," in a waur-o'-the-wear wagonette stood,
ready to convey them to Glentirlie.

The road, on the right, skirted the base of well-rounded,
green, pastoral hills, not high, but sonsie, and sheep-dotted,
which the driver described as "a grand bite—a gude place
—fine feedin'—prime—weel at themsels—top lambs—a
by-ordnar gude hirsel." On the left stretched a meadow
laughing in autumn gladness. Here, was a busy group—the
whole inmates of a small holding, stacking the fragrant
meadow hay ; there the rasp of a cottar's scythe was heard,
followed by the whish of the prostrating " victual." Beyond,

the Tirlie glinted in the sunlight, and brattled along. On the road, sometimes a startled, perplexed, miserable, stray lamb scurried and wheeled dementedly, while its anxious mother watched and bleated at the fence she could not clear; or rabbits hopped across and buried themselves among the furze: and, at one corner, a brace of moorfowl raised their bonnie bodies and plumage from the footpath, stared excitedly, pattered along the road for a short distance in bewilderment, then whirred away, chuckling, into the heather.

The sights and sounds of the country delighted the visitors; the landlord told them the ancient and modern history of the valley. Raeburn was loud in his expressions of pleasure. Baillie rather looked than spoke his feelings. He was taking it all in, and could only spare "beautiful, lovely, grand," as a chorus to his friend's ecstasy, but when they arrived at Glentirlie he summed up his abundant satisfaction in "This will do."

Glentirlie was one of those delightful old roadside inns, which, in the times of mail coaches, post-chaises, and carriers' carts was a busy scene. Its occupation had largely gone since the days of railways, but it had become a resort of well-to-do fishers and sportsmen. There was a fairly-sized farm attached, but nothing of the modern public house or "bar" about the place. When the travellers were shown to their neat bedrooms, where the napery was good old "burn-bleached," home-spun, snow-white linen, and all was fresh and homely, redolent of honeysuckle and wild thyme, they were highly pleased. When they sat down to the substantial "towzie" tea in the big room, the fare was so plain, yet abundant, substantial, and tempting, and Mattie, the servant, so couthie and pleasant, that they felt happy, and Frank could not suppress "three cheers for Glentirlie."

They sauntered out in the evening, first to the burn where the trouts were leaping freely. "That promises well," said Charlie, while Frank proposed to get out the rods and try a "cast." "Let us take in the place first," said Baillie, which they did leisurely. They returned and visited the "steading" "'twixt the gloamin' and the mirk."

While there, "the kye cam' hame," and they enjoyed the embodiment of James Hogg's famous song. When the mirk had settled down, the heavens seemed so much more star-bespangled than they had ever done before, that they gazed upwards and around, entranced by the sparkle, amplitude and glory of the firmament, and were awe-struck and solemn, feeling, as an old writer has expressed, the sense of littleness which hills produce on the spirits in the evening. Charles Baillie quoted many passages appropriate to the scene, and, just before going in for the night, he repeated with great feeling—

> " The stars repeat it down the dark
>   In mystic jewelled light ;
> The Urim and the Thummim
>   In the watches of the night ;
> And strong Orion shouts to me
>   What slumbered in old fable ;
> And echoes from eternal night's vaults
>   Answer—Able—Able.
> And comet cresting bending heavens
>   Waves echo to the word,
> Like waving white plume in the crested
>   Helmet of the Lord."

A walk of about two miles to church on Sabbath morning proved a delight. The rowans, glancing in scarlet and gold, waved about like a banner ; the birds repeated the sweet, ever-fresh, primitive anthem which has delighted all generations of mankind ; the sun gave light or shade to glen and corrie, hill and streamlet ; the world was at rest. When they reached the church, there was the usual " weekly market " near the gate—some shedding flowers over the grave of their loved ones —all Sabbath like.

The opening psalm—

> " I to the hills will lift mine eyes,"

had to them an anthem's force, and, while they enjoyed the whole service, they felt a special appropriateness to the season and autumn surroundings in the closing psalm ; every line

"A WALK OF ABOUT TWO MILES TO CHURCH."

" So Thou the year most lib'rally
    Dost with Thy goodness crown :
And all Thy paths abundantly
    On us drop fatness down.

They drop upon the pastures wide
    That do in deserts lie :
The little hills on every side
    Rejoice right pleasantly.

With flocks the pastures clothed be,
    The vales with corn are clad :
And now they shout and sing to Thee,
    For Thou hast made them glad."

We will not intrude upon their Sabbath privacy. They were wafted backwards to the hallowed associations of well-conducted homes of early days ; nearly forgotten faces, scenes and impressions became vivid, and each

" Lonely man went musing in the fields at even tide,"

but encircled by unseen visitants from the realms of memory, awakening varied thoughts, as if the unseen were real, and the real visionary. When they parted for the evening, they felt that they had spent a day to be remembered.

CHAPTER II.

THIS "Sabbath well spent" had the effect of which Sir Matthew Hale writes as giving " help for the work of the morrow." Merry sounds were heard coming from each room as the old garments were being put on, and these got louder when the young men looked at themselves in the mirrors. The first sight of each other set both off into quizzical laughter, and

the merriment grew noisier as each surveyed himself or his
neighbour.

"Well," said Charlie, when he could speak, "we are
'guys,' and might pass for 'bogles.' If fishing fails, we shall
start as beggars."

When Mattie saw them she laughed heartily and, in her
blunt honesty said, "My certie, gentlemen, ye have made
frichts o' yersels," and reported, on returning to the kitchen,
"that the gentlemen had on as ill-faured claes as ever she saw
on ony tramp; but, for a' that, their bonnie, blythe faces an'
gude manners made them, some way, like real gentlemen too."

The inn and outhouses enclosed a wide courtyard on
three sides, the front being open to the road. Near the
centre stood a primitive wooden pump, the handle of which
was seldom still, and, when in action, it produced quite as
much noise as water.

"That sound awoke me early this morning," said Raeburn.
"I could not make out what the grunting, and squeeling, and
splashing meant."

"Aye," said Mattie; "our pump is like Nannie Henry's
o' Lil's'lie." It has a pitifu' time o't. "We've tried to mak'
it work wi' less noise, but it soon tak's to its auld tune. It's
grand water, an' never rins dry. But I'm sorry it disturbit
you. I'll try and get it sorted."

"Not at all," said Baillie. "It will teach us early hours."

"There's waur lessons," added Mattie. "An' they say
the trouts tak' best in the mornings."

For the first three days the fishers had fair sport in the
near burns, and enjoyed themselves greatly. On Thursday
they tried the "Limpie," a larger stream, about five miles

distant, and were overtaken by a terrific thunderstorm. The shelter of some trees proving useless, they made for an open door in a garden wall, not far from the river. Once inside they darted to a summer-house, but found, to their confusion, two young ladies already there, clinging to each other and quivering with terror. The intruders started and made as if they would retreat; at the same moment an intensely vivid flash, followed by a near, crashing peal, drew from one of the ladies a suppressed scream. The other said, " Don't go. Take what shelter the place gives ;" the more timid lady adding, " Oh! do stay till this fearful storm is past. Ask them please, Fanny, not to leave us here alone."

The storm left no alternative. The rain poured as it *can* and *does* in an upland valley ; flash succeeded flash, peal answered to peal. Baillie offered to go for wraps, but the pelting torrent made that unwise, although he said, and keenly felt, he " had nothing on that would spoil." Indeed, strange as it may seem, the awe naturally produced by such a storm seemed to affect the young men less than would have been expected. When Charlie spoke about "nothing on that would spoil," Raeburn, sighing, said to himself, " I wish we had." They sought the darkest corner of the summer-house, seemed anxious to get behind each other, but somehow could not hit it—stroked their chins, and winced at their unshaven roughness—felt " asses " in not bringing their " tweeds " when coming such a distance—looked ruefully on the garb they had lately laughed heartily at. The missing buttons, boasted of a week ago, were sadly missed now. Both felt ill at ease, but needlessly, for the ladies, huddled closely together, buried their faces on each other's shoulders, overawed by the elemental war, and only half conscious that others shared their shelter and danger.

A lull enabled Charles Baillie to see the mansion-house. He darted off, saying, "Stay, Frank, I'll fetch wraps." Frank would have been off too, had not a timid voice said, "Oh! do stay one of you!" Before Charlie reached the house the storm broke out afresh, but at the door he found an elderly gentleman in a state of great excitement, who anxiously asked, "Have you seen two young ladies?"

"They are in the summer-house, and safe; my companion is with them."

"Thank God," was the fervent reply.

"I will gladly take haps and umbrellas."

"Not yet, not now," said a lady from the front room, "Come in and tell us exactly how they are."

"I am dripping all over," replied Baillie. "They are quite sheltered from the rain, and as composed as could be expected. It seems abating;" and, as the servants appeared with cloaks and umbrellas, he started with a huge armful, saying, "I will fetch them whenever they dare venture." The lull continuing, the ladies were hurriedly, and, dare we say, clumsily muffled up by the young men. They were new to the business and a little nervous, while the ladies were excited and flurried. Baillie started for the house with one under his care; before they had gone half-way the storm raged afresh, Fanny clutched him in terror, but walked firmly. Raeburn followed instantly with the more timid of the two, who grasped him convulsively; indeed, he had almost to carry her. And oft-times, in after years, the two spoke of the courage and thrill with which these terrified grasps inspired them.

Hearty thanks were rained upon the two heroes, which, they said, were quite uncalled for.

Hospitality was urgently pressed upon them, but they could not be persuaded to leave the lobby, giving as a reason their dripping garments. Baillie was honest enough to check *himself*, when saying dripping. Dry clothing was offered, but Frank's fancy pictured how his old "rig" would look at a stranger's kitchen fire, and what conclusions it might suggest. They pled the danger of wet clothes, in which the lady of the house feelingly but reluctantly acquiesced; that the storm might break out afresh, swollen rivers, ignorant of the locality, anxiety about their absence, &c.

They were allowed to depart, not before they had discovered that there was a committee-and-club acquaintanceship between Mr Melville and themselves; that, in society phrase, they knew *about*, if they did not know each other. The fishers promised to lunch at Dunlimpie on Saturday, Mr Melville placing at their disposal his preserved water. Mrs Melville impressed upon them the necessity of going straight home, and getting a "dry change;" and, just as they were leaving, Miss Melville came tripping down stairs, and thanked them heartily in her own name, and that of her cousin Lucy (who desired to be excused owing to a headache), for their presence and help.

The two started homewards, tramped over soft roads, staggered through swollen burns, but the storm had passed and the sun shone clearly. In the course of their walk, an artist looked up from his easel as they passed, and hailing them, offered to give them what would pay their night's lodgings, if they would stand till he sketched them. They

winced, thanked him, and moved on, thinking much, but
saying little.

When they reached Gentirlie, they quickly carried out Mrs
Melville's motherly suggestions, and each looked ruefully at
the moist heap of old body companions, to which they now
bade farewell, with less regret than they would have thought
possible a week ago. Baillie muttered something like
"childish—a mistake—a fiasco." Frank put his foot firmly
on the heap, and said "tomfoolery—all very well, but—
'pay night's lodgings.' Mountebanks in earnest."

Each quietly told Mattie to clear out the old clothes and
give them away. Her reply was blunt but telling.

"If I can get ony body to tak them; if no, they'll make
grand scrubbing claiths. I didna like ye wi' them. It's a'
very weel to gang gizzartin' at an odd time, but ye werena
wise-like, and ye may be glad that ye didna get into company
that wad a' made ye think black burnin' shame o' your haveral
fancy. There's a gude midst in a' thing, an' past that's
neither safe nor fendible."

Little did Mattie think that she was treading heavily on
sore corns, or that her auditors felt that no one could have
expressed their sentiments and experience better. Each recollected some important business requiring him to return to
town. Neither said it was as much a matter of wardrobe as
of business, but "Dawtie" and the railway together brought
them to Edinburgh by an early train on Friday.

They did not rush to their chambers, as men on important
business usually do. By different routes they reached the
hairdresser's together, and wanted "not much off but nicely
trimmed." They also met accidentally at a clothier's, each

wishing a knickerbocker suit, CERTAIN in the afternoon. Of
course the man of cloth "was afraid," "hardly time," but
suddenly recollected suits, ordered for gentlemen out of town
for some time; and the extra guinea he charged consoled him
for the "fear of disappointing good customers." They spent
some time in their "apartments" (where they appeared to the
surprise of their landladies), and packed their portmanteaus as
if for a long and special journey. They found "will return
at 3.30" stuck on the door of their "chambers," walked
off as if the *important* business did not lie there, and reached
Glentirlie in the evening.

At the tea-table they appeared in their new suits, greatly
to Mattie's delight. "Ye're like yoursels now, gentlemen; I
like ye in thae claes. If I was a man I wad gie ye the
'tailor's nip.' I tried three tramps wi' your auld duds, but
they wadna tak' them, so I got the young shepherd to put
them into the pitatie field at the back o' the house for 'tattie
bogles.'"

In their evening walk they recognised the venerable garments doing duty as scarecrows, but the hats were exchanged,
and, (this is private), they filled their new pockets with stones,
and put a few marks of wear on their suits, to take away
the fresh look, for which Mattie all but scolded them as
"menseless craturs, spoilin' their new claes a'ready."

"THE VENERABLE GARMENTS DOING DUTY AS SCARECROWS."

CHAPTER III.

CHARLES BAILLIE and Frank Raeburn were well-built, muscular, handsome, young fellows; the knickerbockers set off their sturdy persons and limbs. When they reached Dunlimpie they were cordially received at the doorstep by Mr Melville, and in the parlour by the ladies of the household, where they were warmly thanked by Mrs Melville, and each by the lady he had "rescued." Fanny making Baillie blush by her bright heartiness, and her cousin, Lucy Crawford, set Frank's heart "a-dunting" as she praised his courage and kindness, while a tear trembled in her eye. Poor Frank was struck dumb, Baillie stammered out, "It was nothing at all —a pleasure—they were the indebted parties for the shelter," and, in a very short time, all felt like old friends.

The fishers seemed in no hurry to go to the preserved water. There was a talk about the storm, and some damage done by the lightning to an old tree, prized for the odd reason that it bore the name of the "gallows tree" of Dunlimpie; and, as the day was fine, the tree was visited, and Baillie's knowledge of botany incidentally revealed, which led to a walk through the garden.

Mr Melville and Fanny had many questions to ask him regarding various shrubs and flowers that had long puzzled them. Baillie knew these well, and explained each minutely.

Frank, spying his old shelter, and not being interested in botany, said to Miss Crawford,

"Charlie is on one of his hobby-horses, and off at the gallop, he is an eminent botanist."

" That will delight Uncle and Fanny; they have several rare plants and varieties they cannot find out about."

" And will equally delight Charlie. It will be something very unusual if he does not know the name, nature, and ' habitat' of every plant he sees, giving long names to common weeds. I know him of old. Start him on botany with a good listener (not my forte), and farewell fishing and everything else. Would you object to show me our old shelter, the summer-house?" And without waiting for a reply, he walked into it.

No one seemed to have been there since the storm, for on the floor lay the joint fishing pocket-book of the two fishers. Frank looked at it, Miss Crawford picked it up, hoping " they did not miss it yesterday." Frank was tickled at not having missed it either yesterday or that morning, and said, " We were not fishing yesterday," adding internally, " for various good reasons."

" See how pleased Uncle and Fanny are," said Lucy, brightly. " Your friend seems to have solved, or to be solving, a question that has puzzled every one they have consulted. Uncle will be delighted." And she told that he was her mother's brother; that her father had been an Admiral in the Royal Navy; that father and mother were dead; that Uncle and Aunt were *both* to her, and if possible more; and that Fanny was so bright and clever, that she often felt ashamed of herself being so stupid.

" I don't like clever people," said Charlie; " well, not quite that, I am sometimes afraid of them, or rather ashamed of myself before them, which I am sure you need never be. Yet Frank Raeburn and I are the best of friends, and in his absence I have no hesitation in calling him a noble, upright, clever fellow."

At the close of Charles Baillie's explanation about a rare and curious plant, Miss Melville, looking about, said, " Where is your friend ? "

" I saw Frank make for the summer-house, which did him and me such a good turn the other day. He has not much patience with the exact sciences, but is as shrewd a fellow on many other matters as is in Edinburgh, as genuine as ever breathed—good-heartedness embodied."

The bell for luncheon cut short conversation which had incidentally led the young men to speak of one another, but at table each justified the other's words. All found they had many friends in common, and a distant Scotch cousinship was partly unravelled between Mrs Melville and Frank Raeburn, for the three botanists formed one group, and Mrs Melville, Lucy, and Charlie another.

" There is another plant or two I should like your opinion about," said Mr Melville, rising, " but I must not keep you from fishing."

" I should like to see the plant," said Baillie.

" I am not particular about fishing," added Raeburn.

" Perhaps the gentlemen would like to visit Kilcoungo," said Mrs Melville.

" Kilcoungo ? " said Baillie. " Is it a Culdee or a Catholic foundation ? From the terminology ' oungo ' it seems Culdee, for they had Mungos and Beugos and Bungos and Cadzows. By all means let us go there—is it far ? Can't we all go ? "

" You seem to have got on *your* hobbyhorse now," said

Miss Crawford. " It is little more than a mile distant, but not in the direction of the best fishing——"

" That's no matter. There is an old legend of an early saint coming to Scotland from Cong in Ireland, but his cell is not known. Let us all go;" and in a few minutes they were walking up a pretty glen, with sides so steep that the gentlemen had to assist the ladies in rugged places. On reaching a broad, open space, Frank's practised eye picked out what seemed the site of an old chapel or cell, and on examination he found several interesting evidences of its antiquity, and of tumuli around it. Baillie also found some rare ferns, mosses, and ancient medicinal herbs. Mr Melville was delighted, and proposed that next week the interior should be cleaned out and examined, which was readily agreed to. The " preserved water " was again referred to, but the day was so bright and the surroundings so tempting, that the party rambled and climbed, enjoying distant views and fairy nooks. Dinner-hour had arrived before they got back to Dunlimpie; the visitors were easily prevailed on to join the party, and all went " merry as a marriage bell."

Our heroes reached Glentirlie in high glee, and Mattie " was glad they had been 'sae weel put on,' for Dunlimpie was a real gentleman, and the young ladies awfu' nice. It was a gude thing they found out that young Goldie and Walker were just gamblers. They stayed here a while, and it was aye bet-bettin' an' wagerin', an' ither kinds o' bad conduct. It gied the young leddies a sair heart at the time, but it was a providential escape. They're owre't noo. Nae leddies deserve better men, and nae men could get better wives." The gentlemen quite agreed with her, and thought

a good deal about Dunlimpie and its denizens ever there-
after.

The ransacking of Kilcoungo took two days. Several
antiquarian treasures were found: old cists, pieces of primitive
pottery, stone or flint weapons, besides broken fonts and
other evidences of ancient saintship. Frank reserved his full
opinion until he had consulted some authorities, and compared
the relics with others in the Antiquarian Museum. Mr
Melville felt sure that the place had been an early church,
for the fathers always selected the cosiest place in the district.
Baillie suggested that they should meet Frank at the museum,
to which all agreed. Again the "preserved water" was un-
visited, for the garden of Dunlimpie kept Baillie and Miss
Melville fully occupied, while Frank and Miss Crawford pre-
ferred the summer-house, Mr Melville alternately botanizing
with the former and sitting beside the latter, anxious to con-
firm his idea that there was a real, ancient, ecclesiastical edifice
on his estate of Dunlimpie.

The visit to the Antiquarian Museum was duly paid.
Frank's thorough knowledge of its contents surprised Baillie,
and delighted the others. They formerly had thought the
place dry and musty, but now it teemed with interest. They
found ample evidence that Kilcoungo was a real Culdee's cell,
and some of the "finds" indicated its existence for over a
thousand years.

The young men were occasional, almost regular (some
people said frequent) visitors at Mr Melville's town house—
Frank being a special favourite of Mrs Melville's, because he
was always ready to be a *fourth* at whist, allowing Mr
Melville and Baillie to discuss trees, and plants, and flowers.

The young folks often met accidentally (?) in the Royal Academy's Exhibition, and, for a time, Frank and Miss Melville studied, at least talked about the pictures, while Charles and Lucy walked quietly round, but said little. Fanny told Lucy that Mr Raeburn rattled on so fast she was confused, Lucy that Mr Baillie was so quiet she felt awkward. Next time they met in the Academy the ladies changed partners, to the great delight of all, for Baillie was carried away by Miss Melville's pat catching of the artistic hits, while Lucy was charmed with Raeburn's happy knack of making the bits glow and tell. That night Fanny told Lucy that she did like Mr Baillie, and Lucy, kissing her fondly, said, "So do I Mr Raeburn." If the young men had overheard them it would have saved them many an anxious thought.

Charles Baillie sedately reasoned the matter out—whether to ask Miss Melville or her father first; he thought the former best, but prepared himself for either. They met, accidentally really, in a railway carriage—the distance was short—between Waverley and Haymarket Stations, Edinburgh. As the train started a lightning flash, followed by a terrific peal, made Miss Melville start and involuntarily cling to Baillie; when they came out at Haymarket Station he had her sanction to "ask papa;" and, at rather a late hour that evening he burst into Frank Raeburn's apartments, and without preface, said, "Frank, I am engaged to Fanny Melville." Frank all but hugged him: "Bravo! Bless you! Bless her! Bless you both!! You are a lucky fellow—again, bless you both!!" Then looking ruefully (a new aspect for him), he said, "Frank, I have Lucy Crawford on the brain—she's—

she's—she's—tuts, I'm raving—I don't think I could make her happy—I do not deserve her."

"Neither do *I* Fanny," said Baillie; "but *she* thinks otherwise. Why don't you try Lucy?"

"I have schemed, and thought, and wondered, and resolved, and wished, but the more I do the more I shrink: she's such a—tuts!—and I am such a—a—a—"

"Excuse slang, Frank—'a duffer.' You could make Miss Crawford happier than any man on earth, and she would make you——"

"Stop, Charlie; don't tantalise me."

"I will not stop, Frank; you used to be the rattle, and I the slow coach. Come along with me to-morrow night, and congratulate Miss Melville (if you can). You may get a quiet chat with Miss Crawford."

The "chat" proved quiet enough: for, very shortly after he had congratulated Miss Melville, she and Charlie withdrew, not before Fanny had said, "Mr Raeburn, I feel so happy that I wish Lucy was in a similar position," and Charlie had said, "Ditto, for my doubting friend Raeburn."

It would be unpardonable to intrude too much on the perplexed couple. Frank spoke about Kilcoungo and Dunlimpie, and the summer-house—Miss Crawford added in joke, "and the preserved fishings."

Frank laughed almost sadly, and abruptly said, "Miss Crawford"—then he paused, blushed, and jerked out—"What a lucky fellow Baillie is, he has fished to purpose. I wish I could hope for equal luck. Dare I—excuse me, Miss Crawford, but dare I—ask you to make me as happy—as Charlie is——"

Lucy hung her head, was silent for a while, then whispered, " Yes, Frank dear, if aunt and uncle consent."

Baillie was in ecstacies for some time, then the serious matter of asking aunt and uncle's consent appalled him.

Fanny relieved him of the trying ordeal, and, at the supper table, Frank sat beside Lucy Crawford as his affianced bride. Lucy Melville, although only a day in advance, felt quite at home with Charlie. Mrs Melville made stringent conditions that she was to have a visit from both after their marriage, at least once a week, and Mr Melville felt much alone, yet very highly pleased.

We need not linger over what remains of our story. Marriage presents flowed in, until Mrs Melville's drawing-room was like an exhibition. One, however, must have honourable mention. About a fortnight before the marriage, Captain Webber and Lieutenant O'Hara were announced as wishing to see Miss Crawford, and, following the servant who announced them, right into the dining-room, they bowed all round, then, addressing Miss Crawford, presented her, in the name of those who had served under her father, the dear, old Admiral, with a gold anchor, glittering in diamonds and emeralds, and with a superabundance of gold chain.

Captain Webber, a thorough English tar, hoped "that her joys would be as deep as the ocean, and her sorrows as light as its spray."

Lieutenant O'Hara, a genuine Irishman, wished "that their path would be strewn with roses as they walked, hand in hand, over the stormy ocean of life." The tars joined the supper table, and spun yarns about the good old Admiral till a late or early hour.

Not infrequently Frank and Charlie met in "houses to let," once or twice in those to "sell;" but why prolong our tale further than to tell that they had grand times of it at Dunlimpie during the season. The summer-house was a favourite resort, but only two were in it at one time. The "preserved water" was visited, strolled about, but not fished. Mattie of Glentirlie was promoted to be housekeeper, almost companion, to Mrs Melville, after the young couples had started on the honeymoon; and often, when they visited either town or country house, she reminded the gentlemen of the scarecrows in the potato field at Glentirlie.

John Tod

A Ballade of Tobacco Smoke

WHAT fretting loads we mortals bear
  Through life, whose fading rainbows mock,
And Time who drives a splendid pair
  Of steeds he never will unyoke,
Sweeps his lean fingers through our hair,
  He scarcely leaves a decent lock,
Yet chide him not, if still he spare
  The dreams seen through tobacco smoke.

We each must have our little care
  To add by contrast to our joke,
A laugh that spreads in vain its snare
  To catch the lips of solemn folk.
Well, let us walk through all the fair,
  And watch the crowds that sway and shock ;
They follow what we see elsewhere —
  The dreams seen through tobacco smoke.

Dreamers of dreams in ships of air,
  Whose keels have never enter'd dock,
I wish you may have sounder ware
  Than did Alnaschar when he woke !
Statesmen, when strife is high, forswear
  For half-an-hour the wordy stroke,
I fain would hint of better fare —
  The dreams seen through tobacco smoke !

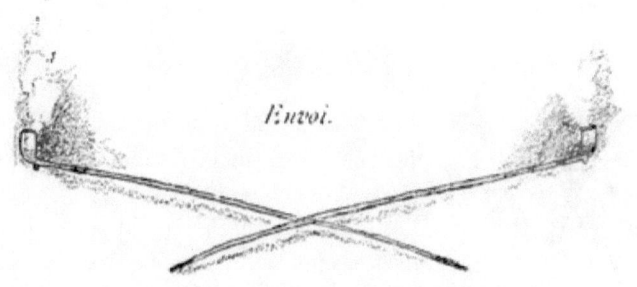

Envoi.

Prince, when you weary of the chair
  From which you govern realms and folk,
Your faithful bard would have you share
  The dreams seen through tobacco smoke!

A. Anderson

A Sunny Morning in my Garden

HAT dependent creatures we are after all! Nature has us in thrall, and in her changing moods can make of us what she will!

How bright the world and all its uses seems on a morning such as this, when it is a perfect gladness to be alive!

The sun has been up for hours, and his progress is most royal. He brooks no barrier in his way, there is not even the fleeciest film of summer cloud to dim his splendour. Matchless and radiant is the sky, and blue, blue the summer sea. The little waves break yonder on the pebbly shore, with scarcely a murmur or a sigh.

But I am at my south window to-day, and am looking out upon my garden, to me a pleasant place, although beginning now to wear the pensive grace of autumn.

You who revel in ancestral parks and walk proudly among your gay parterres, would smile in mild derision at my little garden, but I question if your lordly pleasaunce is a source of as real delight to you as this tiny provincial strip is to me. It is veritably a strip, with a straight and solemn path dividing it. You can take it all in at one glance, and count the blossoms without difficulty, but though it is small and narrow, and altogether beneath your contempt, it is full of friendliness and honesty and good purposes for me. Of course it is not my ideal: from the recesses of tenderest memory I will draw you a picture which represents the garden of my childhood. It was very long and wide, with a low mossy wall running all round it, and a little green wicket gate so little used that it creaked always on its hinges. It was intersected all through by shady, grassy walks under the shade of gnarled and laden apple trees: it had great untidy fantastic flower beds, shut in by borders of boxwood grown nearly as high as a hedge. Do

you know what grew in these beds? Perhaps you know some cottage garden which will furnish the almost forgotten names —mint and rosemary and thyme, bachelor's buttons and southernwood and nancy-pretty, Canterbury bells, lupins and tiger lilies; nothing fine or rare or conspicuously lovely, yet we loved them all.

I have not seen that old garden, though it is not very remote, these many years: memory is sweeter than the vision of a change which may be. Strange feet now step across the threshold of the old house, and strange hands perhaps have made the green wicket swing silently to and fro.

Many were wont to laugh at our old garden, and to say banteringly it grew splendid weeds, but though it had not the vestige of respectability about it, the hearts of children, now scattered far and wide, have memories of it wholly sacred.

Memory is always with us, and silently, day by day, we add to her storehouse. Although she has some bitter roots among her bundle of herbs, what would life be without her sweet companionship? How awful if our happy days departed from us at sunset wholly and utterly, as if they had never been; how barren and arid then would be the desert of existence! Memory, then, we constantly bless and cherish, growing more anxious as we step on and upward that we should sow what will give us a harvest such as shall not make us ashamed.

The heart clings persistently to earliest memory; how important then that those who have children to care for should make these early days conspicuously bright.

Oh! there is enough awaiting these young hearts, enough spirit-anguish and heart-weariness to satisfy the grimmest mentor. Let them at least have sunshine gilding that childhood which is never forgotten.

Am I moralising too seriously in my garden this sunny morning? Well, well; there is nothing incongruous between the brightness of this sweet day, and my plea for the children's happy environment. So we come back quite naturally to where we began, that nature is a great deal to us, and has something comforting and strengthening for us in our most wayward moods.

She is very gentle with us too; her touch when sorrows fall thick and fast upon us is divinest healing. She has her merry moods likewise, but she reveals herself only to those who love her, and seek to commune with her. And that communion is not exclusive or difficult of access, but is open always to the seeking eye and ear, the sympathetic mind, and the simple, earnest heart. This sympathy with nature brings to the human heart courage and forbearance and loving-kindness with an understanding of simple goodness which makes life a perpetual joy.

Annie S. Swan

"La Tombe dit à la Rose"

From Victor Hugo.

THE Tomb said to the Rose,
  "Those tears the mornings weep
  Into thy petals deep,
What does love's flower with those?"

The Rose said to the Tomb,
  "And thou, what dost thou—say'—
  With that which day by day
Drops in Thy gulf of gloom?"

The Rose said, "I do this:—
  Out of those tears I make
  A soul of perfume wake—
Honey and ambergris."

"Poor flower," the Tomb said, "I
  Out of each life that slips
  Mute through my earthen lips,
Make a winged soul on high."

W. H. Mallock.

The Truth about Lambs

IN this matter-of-fact nineteenth century it behoves us to guard zealously the little of the poetic which has not been driven away by the demon steam.

My regard for poetry and poets is only exceeded by my love of, and sympathy for, the humid and rheumatic Goddess of Truth, who has been forced to take up her abode in a well; and it is in order to prevent any further waste of sympathy or love on an unworthy object, that I intend telling the truth about lambs.

However unworthy the object on which we place our affection may be, we do not thank those who remove the scales from our eyes; we do not like to see our idol broken, and discover that it is made of clay. I hope, however, that the reader will defer his judgment on me till he has read my experience, when I shall have more hope of being excused, or having my offence palliated.

I can scarcely control myself to speak calmly on the subject, when I think of, or try to imagine, the amount of sympathy and love which has "from time immemorial" been wasted on these unworthy objects; and it is the poets who are principally to blame for rousing our sympathy and affection.

Poets have chosen lambs as the emblems of innocence and peace, and they never were further from the truth.

It grieves me to disturb the proverbs of centuries, to strip the lamb of its false covering, and show up the ignorance of poets.

What do poets know of nature? Thomson wrote of the beauties of a sunrise, when it is well known he usually had breakfast in bed. They have written of "The ploughboy's whistle and the milkmaid's song" as something enchanting, which only shows their utter disregard for truth, or their entire want of an ear for music. I have heard both, and they are extremely vulgar, and I hope to be spared the infliction again. Let a poet sit through a Harvest Home, and he will change his mind, but "revenons à nos moutons."

Last spring I spent a good deal of time in the company of lambs, and my opinion, formed on close observation, is that they are the most selfish, idiotic, discontented, and combative animals on the face of the earth, leaving the following to support my assertion.

When a lamb is about a week old it discovers that its mother is a lunatic, with one idea, and that is its lamb, and instead of returning its mother's love, it abuses it. Another lamb, which we will call *B*, comes to play with lamb *A*, when *A*'s mother, fearing her offspring will be contaminated by such company, knocks over *B* with a box in the ribs. *A* naturally thinks it belongs to a superior set, and condescendingly visits lamb *B*, only to discover that *B*'s mother holds similar opinions about its lamb, this reflection being made by *A* when it is knocked on its back.

A gets up and runs bleating to its mother, and gets a drink, and as the milk gets scarce it digs its mother with its little horns; the mother, thinking it is time to stop, lies down for a rest, when the lamb climbs on her back, planting its sharp little hoofs between its mother's ribs, till the mother has to rise, when the lamb goes for another drink.

A lamb pays no attention to its mother unless it wants a drink, which it usually does every few minutes.

As soon as a lamb can walk straight on its clumsy legs it looks about for a smaller lamb to box, when the smaller lamb is not looking. This is the nearest approach to humour in a lamb's composition.

A lamb's legs look as if they had been made for its big brother, and it is as proud of them as a boy is of his first trousers. It tries to gambol, the result being, like a stool under the influence of spirit rapping, it throws its hind legs a few inches up into the heavens, and fancies it is fit for a circus.

I was beside some sheep in a shed where they had more good turnips and hay than they could eat, and leaving the gate open, they rushed out and ate ravenously at rotten turnips which had been thrown aside as useless. This is the only human trait I have observed in sheep.

After I had been about a week painting a picture of sheep and lambs, I laid down my pallette on the camp stool, and walked out of the shed to have a smoke, and a talk with a young girl who attended to the cows, and was just in the middle of an interesting conversation when she said,

" I think the sheep have knocked over your picture."

I thought she was only saying it to frighten me, but when I did go back I found my easel and canvas flat on the ground, and a lamb on the top of the picture, smelling if it was painted in oil or water colour. I drove them back, making some remarks which I do not remember now, and started to scrape the canvas, when the head of the lamb's mother came into violent collision with me, and I don't believe any artist ever before got through a picture of the size in such a short time, and it was completely finished. At the same time one cannot fail to see the want of anything like justice in that sheep butting me for trying to prevent the lamb from injuring my property.

I hope I have justified my assertion, and if the reader can now enjoy his roast lamb and mint sauce without compunction, I have not lived in vain.

W. Grant Stevenson.

The Beautiful

I.

THE mystery of Loveliness, that lies,
 Like light from some diviner heaven than ours,
  On visible Nature: mountains, streams and
   flowers.
  On man's proud front, in depths of woman's eyes;
  The mystery of Loveliness, that is
 The Law of Nature's being: moulding all—
 The measureless great, the infinitely small—
To its own perfect beauty.   What is this
But the translation of God's inmost thought?
 And that is Love; Nature the mighty scroll
 Whereon 'tis writ.   Thou readest it, my soul!
Each sacred syllable, yet graspest not,
Save in dim gleams, the message written there,
Though questioning evermore in Work and Prayer.

II.

Yet, O my soul! thank God that He hath sent,
In loving answer to thy life-long cry,
 These shadowings of the holier Mystery
Behind the veil—for rapturous moments rent
As by a still, small voice from highest heaven.

If thou with feeble hand and care-clogged brain
  Through life's grey clouds hast groped—alas! in vain—
To catch their import, thou at least hast striven ;
And, striving, won the guerdon ne'er denied
  To those who battle bravely—though they fail.
  For such one day the Angel calm and pale
With tender hand will draw the veil aside,
And they shall stand within the Holy Place,
And read the Secret in The Master's face.

Nör Palm

The Gypsy Wooer

THE young lords rade frae east and west,
  Sae blithe were they and bonny,
And all to court our lady gay,
  For she was best of ony.

The young lords rade to east and west,
  Wi' heavy dule and grieving,
Their hearts were wae, for she said them nay.
  And bade them cease their deaving.

She lookèd frae her bower window,
  The sun it shone sae brightly,
An' over field and over fell
  A gypsy steppit lightly.

The gypsy man cam doun the brae,
  An' clear his pipes were singing
An outland sang as wild and fey
  As Elfin bridles ringing.

O whiles the sang went wud wi' joy,
  And whiles it sorrowed sairly;
The saut tear stood in our lady's ee,
  It rang sae sweet and rarely.

The Gypsy Wooer.

" An' are ye come at last ? " she said,
  " An' do I see and hear ye ?
If this be no my ain true love
  Then nane shall be my dearie.

" An' where hae ye been sae lang ? " quo she,
  " An' why cam ye ne'er before, O !
If ye be no my ain true love,
  My heart will break for sorrow."

O never a word the gypsy said,
  And naething did he linger,
But his een laughed bright as he turned his head,
  And beckoned wi' his finger.

She's casten off her silken snood,
  And taen her mantle to her,
An' she's awa to Silverwood,
  To follow the gypsy wooer.

An Old World Matter

IN the old world of Edinburgh, when the High Street, the Canongate, and the Cowgate, with their adjacent closes, constituted the royal burgh, it was not often that anything occurred to disturb the still and tranquil life of the peace-loving citizens. No visit of royalty had taken place since the time of Charles I. True, the Royal Commissioners walked (literally then) on the opening of the General Assembly; but at the time of which I write, the "walking" or procession of Parliament had long since been discontinued, and Edinburgh, the metropolis of Scotland, could boast of little excitement or bustle beyond that of any provincial city in the kingdom. For all that, many of the old nobility still remained domiciled in the quaint turreted flats that frowned in the moonlight from either side of the High Street, and in the gatherings of the select, the "assemblies," and the weekly "concerts" of the "Musical Society," much blue blood as well as youth, beauty, and intellect gathered together to enliven what must have been, upon the whole, a dull existence. The Pretender, with his ill-equipped followers, passed through the town in 1745. The romance attached to that fatal expedition has already been amply written. What the following brief narrative has to record is but a small matter concerning the history of two people of no more importance than an actress and an actor, who, so far as Edinburgh counted, could certainly boast, after the manner of Cæsar, that they came, were seen, and conquered.

It was in the year 1762 that the *Courant* newspaper announced that "a gentlewoman will appear for the first time on the stage of this kingdom in four plays. Particular tickets (at the usual prices) will be printed, as no money will be received at the door." Such was the first announcement of the beautiful and fascinating Mrs Bellamy who, in London, had secured for herself at once a fame and a notoriety that have seldom been equalled, even in the annals of the stage.

Fresh from the whirl of London excitement the previous year, she had visited Dublin, and there she met West Digges, an actor who, in addition to great personal recommendations, was possessed of genuine histrionic ability. She had been warned against Digges' persuasive tongue and insinuating manners; but, possibly for that very reason, all the sooner succumbed to the blandishments of a gentleman who had almost no equal in the power of persuading. While in Dublin they lived together happily enough; but for some strange reason Mrs Bellamy had a strong dislike to Scotland, and swore (ladies did swear in those days) she would never act in that country. This she did, no doubt, knowing that Digges was co-lessee in the Edinburgh Theatre. He, however, was manager first and lover second, and so contrived to get her transported to Edinburgh without her knowing where she was being taken to. Entering the town she enquired where she was? to which the ready response came—"the Grassmarket," and in the simpleness of her soul she thought such was the name of a town. She was driven to a lodging in the Canongate, and while combing her hair a sound of music saluted her

ears. " What is that sound?" she cried. " The theatre," replied her maid. At once seeing she had been trapped, she
seized a pair of scissors and cut all her hair off quite close
to her head, in order that she might be unable to appear.
Such was the impulsive character of the lady, so it is not sur-
prising that Digges soon persuaded her (no doubt after a
stormy interview) to appear in the plays for which she had
already been advertised. A wig supplied the place of the
demolished hair, and a greater or more fashionable event in the
local theatrical world had never been witnessed than her first
appearance. The highest of the land filled the pit, while the
boxes were packed with the first ladies in society, and it is
said the servants in attendance were so many that they could
not find room in the gallery—a portion of the house then
exclusively reserved for such gentry.

During her stay in Edinburgh Mrs Bellamy was *fêted* far
beyond any actress who had preceded her. Everything
that she could possibly want was hers if she only expressed a
wish to have it; yet her old character of improvidence never
forsook her, and when she was on the eve of leaving Edinburgh for Glasgow, where a theatre had been specially built
for her to appear in, she found she had no money, and sent
her maid to pawn a beautiful gold repeater which Digges
had presented to her. The maid, luckless woman, took it
to the identical watchmaker from whom it had been pur-
chased not many days previously, *but not paid for*, and was
immediately taken into custody. Mrs Bellamy remained
sitting in her carriage for over an hour for the return of her
messenger, until guessing what had happened, she drove to
one of the Lords of Session, her friend, who not only gave
her sufficient money, but got the girl instantly released, and

so enabled this charming actress, but frail woman, to proceed
to Glasgow, where alas she found that the theatre which had
been specially built for her to appear in, had been burnt to
the ground the previous evening, by some over-zealous
bigots of the Methodist persuasion, in obedience to the desires
of their preacher, who had announced to them that he had
seen a vision commanding them to commit arson.

The course of true love between Digges and Bellamy did
not long run smooth. The following season they took a house
in Bonnington (still standing), then an outlying village,

which had to be reached by way of the Horse Wynd, Low
Calton, and Leith Walk, then a dismal country road or track.

The only mode of conveyance was in chairs, very unsafe indeed, considering the roads were of the roughest, the "bearers"
seldom of the soberest, and the chance of meeting footpads
not by any means remote. At Bonnington the twain lived in
great luxury, but family feuds were not uncommon. One
night the argument ran so high that Digges stripped off the
most of his clothes and ran from the house with the intention
of drowning himself in a pond near to the house. Mrs
Bellamy surveyed the proceeding with the utmost coolness,
and when he made his exit, calmly locked the door. The

result may be guessed, for the cold east wind and snow soon made the gentleman change his mind and repent his haste; but when he returned and found the door barred against him, it was only by going down on his naked knees on the snow, and swearing all sorts of repentance, that he gained admittance at last to the cheerful glow of the fire, perhaps more essential under the circumstances than even the smiles and caresses of the authoress of his affliction, which, by the way, he certainly never deserved and never after secured. *Sic transit gloria mundi.*

Jas C Dowdw

MR. DIGGES IN THE CHARACTER OF SIR JOHN BRUTE.

"GONE, GET YOU GONE UP STAIRS."

Men and Books

" The proper study of mankind is man."—Pope

THE gods make living poems ; what we write
   Is photograph, unreal shadowy stuff ;
Their words have wings of power and thews of might,
Ours float like mist, and vanish with a puff.
There are who love to pore o'er musty books,
Scholars, who heap up stores of printed breath,
And spell with painful care and peeping looks
The quaint memorial blazonry of death.
But let me read God's best of living books,
The rosy child, with eyes of trustful blue,
The lightfoot youth, the girl with radiant looks,
Or, like thee, Gordon, the brave captain, who
Leaps into danger, and sublimely rash,
Turns panic into victory with a flash !

John Stuart Blackie

The Prayer of the Pompeian Mother

OH! spare my child, ye Gods who dwell on high!
    Ye gave him unto me :--my only joy,
Oh! rain not ashes on my darling boy.
Hear me, great Zeus, hear a mother's cry,
For his dead father's sake let him not die ;
Hear from his boyish lips the piteous cries !
Shield us from trembling ground, from falling skies,
Cease but a moment, that we both may fly
This choking sand, these reeling rocks and trees :
Return once more thy sweet and balmy breeze,
So that our parchèd tongues again may raise
Before thy altar, songs of love and praise :
Send us again the cheering light of heaven,
And to thy service shall his life be given.

D. W. Steven

THE POMPEIAN MOTHER
SHIELDING HER CHILD FROM THE SHOWER OF ASHES.
A.D. 79.

FROM THE GROUP BY
D. W. STEVENSON, R.S.A.

An Easterly Harr

WE who have been dwellers in the East,—not the picturesque East of palm trees, camels and caravans, but the bleak East of our own little kingdom,—know what an easterly harr means, and we have been told on good authority where the visitor comes from. From the low lands of Holland the visitor travels to our coast, we are assured; and we can believe it. We are not so well informed with regard to the origin of our enemy's name, though it is a singularly expressive and suitable name; for while the thing itself is dim and misty, soft and fleecy, with a certain impalpability in its fleeciness, it has a rough edge; it grates in the throat and the chest; it cuts and pricks with a saw-like jaggedness which answers exactly to its strange title, to the two "r's" that end the word, which we pronounce with an emphatic zest, as a Northumbrian rattles his bur, "har-r."

The season of the year when the harr was most apt to descend upon us was "the sweet spring time:" a time not quite so sweet in the north and the east as in the south and the west, yet glad exceedingly in the lengthening daylight, the budding trees and hedges, the sprouting grass, the first lamb, the first daisy—a time all the brighter to the young and hale because it was keenly bracing in its brightness.

Even so late as the month of May, during the General Assembly of the representatives of its national Churches,

when its streets, old and new, swarm with black coats, the grey metropolis of the north is not unacquainted with easterly harrs. But the Dutch invader recurs to our memory chiefly as it was wont to assail "country sides," when the young wheat showed a fresh, green braird in fields near the sea, above which the lark sang long before the bells of the golden cowslips nodded in the chill breeze over the pasture, or the primroses did more than lift up their meek, pale faces in the garden-borders.

The infliction had a habit of presenting itself at any hour. It started with the sun, and rendered his beams watery and wan. After a bright morning, it fell upon us at high noon like a wet blanket, and shrouded the landscape for the rest of the day. It rose with a ghostly wraith-like appearance, and obscured the full moon. It was always densest nearest the sea, but it did not disdain to stretch a considerable distance inland, creeping on with a stealthy motion, or suddenly descending after the fashion of the drop-scene of a theatre. It hid man and beast; especially beast,—for a dog rashly running ahead disappeared in it, as if a cloud had come between the creature and his owner. Birds of the air were not only invisible, they became mute as fishes in the sea, under the influence of an easterly harr; indeed, it was a singularly muffling, dulling process in nature resembling, so far, the hush of a snow-storm.

The harr clung in a close, white drapery to trees; it swallowed up houses; it obliterated hills. Standing on the shore, the presence of a boat was only known by the splash of the oars. Plodding along the Queen's highway, or stumbling over the deep ruts in a bye-road, the approach of a

cart, or of one of the gigs of the day, or of a man or boy on
horse-back, was not to be detected save by the rattle of the
wheels, and the beat of the horses' feet.   Such moving
figures, looming gigantic in the magnifying medium, came in
sight, and vanished with the astonishing celerity of a
dissolving view.   The commonest objects borrowed a weird
aspect from an easterly harr.

    Dutch courage was wanted to face the " Hollander," for

it froze the marrow in your bones, caused your breath to
labour, hung your garments with drops of moisture, as of the
heaviest night-dews.   But it met you straight in the face, and
was even puritanically fair and clean.   Who, that has ever
encountered the murky abominations of a London fog, with
the solid vileness of its pea-soup atmosphere, and its effect
as of jaundice on every face exposed to it, would not choose

a thousand times, in preference, the sharpest bite of an easterly harr.

Then, as a rule, the reign of the foe did not last long—it went as unexpectedly as it came. It was gone before you knew where you were or it was. The winding-sheet, wrapping all creation in its folds, was transformed in the twinkling of an eye to a nun's veil, modest and demure. In another moment it too was changed. The sun's rays flashed forth and lit it up with silver radiance. It was no longer a sober vestal's veil, it was the veil of a blushing bride, ready to be flung back that she might receive the kiss of her eager bridegroom. For it is true that—

> "Old earth is fair, and fruitful and young,
> And her bridal-day will come ere long."

Sarah Tytler.

The Poppy Blows

THE careful farmer ploughs and hoes :
　　The weeds he slays with ceaseless pains.
And every idle flower that grows.
　　Broadcast he sows his chosen grains ;
　　His harvests whiten o'er the plains,
Still in his wheat the poppy blows.

Forth to the world the prophet goes ;
　　Of wrath and sin and grief he plains,
To careless hearts denouncing woes :
He damns the worldling and his shows.
　　A rich reward for him remains ;
Yet in his wheat the poppy blows.

So He the human heart that sows,
  Untiring, with His golden grains,
  Truth, Virtue, Love, with ceaseless pains,
So vainly, often, —well He knows!—
  How patient that Great Heart remains,
Though in His wheat the poppy blows!

"The Castled Rhine"

" Spake full well, in language quaint and olden,
One who dwelleth by the Castled Rhine."
— LONGFELLOW.

WE are on the Rhine—the beautiful Rhine at last! All the freshness of early summer is on the vine-clad hills and waving forests. The cuckoo still rings his queer note out from some ravine or leafy glade. If the Rhine country can ever look less than lovely, it is surely not in June! And we two islanders, who, free from desk and drudgery, stand to-day under an awning on board the good *Dampfschiff* "Schiller," as it speeds up the shining river, are naturally in the very best of humours for appreciating it all, since this is the crowning holiday we have been looking forward to for years. What does it matter to us that everybody else seems to have "done" the Rhine?—that Brown, Jones, and Robinson, with their respective spouses and families, declare it to be hackneyed and over-rated? " A nice enough run, you know! Pleasant scenery, and no end of old castles; all that sort of thing, certainly, but not a bit fresher than the Clyde!" Well, perhaps it isn't, but it may be worth seeing for all that, surely; so let them say any disagreeable things that occur to them, by all means! *We* have *not* seen the Rhine!

I have called it a holiday, but it is a holiday with certain limitations. For what means that pile of books my comrade lugs along with him at every turn, as if his personal safety depends on the same? They mean for *me* a considerable amount of work,—steady, absorbing, persevering work! For my friend takes out his sketch-book, calmly remarking that it will take all his valuable time to catch an outline here and there, and so it will be as well if I take Baedekker in hand, and also look up the maps as we go along, if I don't mind! Of course I have to say that "I don't mind," and I bend cheerfully to my task. But there is not only Baedekker, but a large selection of minor guide-books that have to be compared therewith, and a set of huge, unfolding maps that persist in fluttering wildly in the breeze, whenever you look them up, in the most exasperating manner. Before the first hour is over, what a flood of ancient history I have had to wade through! From the days of Julius Cæsar downwards, there is not a moment of repose for the earnest and enquiring tourist. He must face the iron legions and the conquering eagles, crusading armies and marauding bands. No wonder if he turn sometimes with a sigh of relief to the bit of love-story, legend, or fairy-lore, Baedekker inserts as a sort of padding here and there. The student sadly needs some such refreshment. He finds something life-like and interesting in the two brother-knights who so provokingly fall in love with the very same lady! She is a lady, however, whose beauty and fascinations are sufficient to account for any number of knights falling in love with her at the same time.

How vivid, too, is the picture of the rash female who per-

sists in rushing off to a convent—of the very strictest kind,
of course, from which she can never again emerge—on hear-
ing some malicious *on dit* from Syria of her absent lover's
faithlessness or death. No warrior is so safe to turn up
again as *that* warrior. Don't we feel the most comfortable
assurance that before we turn the page again Roland will be
standing before us on the very ledge of the rock where his
father's castle still stands? And don't we know for certain
that, however much appearances may have been against him,
the languishing looks of Syrian belles have had no power over
him, his heart having been with his adored Hildegunde all
the time? Here, however, hope and comfort end. We
know only too well that it is "all up" with Hildegunde.
The lady abbess will never let her out of her clutches in
this world. All that remains for her Roland is to stand
staring down from that beetling cliff overhanging the convent
—where, however, he has the prudence to build a neat stone
edifice to shelter him in cold weather—until one mournful
day the tolling of the convent bell shall announce to him
that his beloved Hildegunde is no more. How he knows
that it *is* Hildegunde, and not one of the ordinary sisters,
is a question that occurs to me as I read, but to which
Baedekker gives no response. Perhaps he doesn't know
himself!

It is in this species of study that much of my time
has been spent this morning, and pleasant as it sounds,
I don't know that I have worked harder among books,
history, and dates in particular since my school-days. But
to proceed.

It is said that there were originally sixty-six castles on

"THE CASTLED RHINE."

the Rhine, and of the residue we have already passed a
goodly number, still perched jauntily enough upon their airy
crags for all that time and warfare have done to destroy
them.   And we have gazed on the "Seven Mountains," a
grand unfolding panorama, a blending of the lovely and the
sublime, with the haunted "DRACHENFELS" as its crowning
glory. Also we have seen Bonn the old university town
and the pleasant modern residence, and dozens of little
villages dotting the green shores with mountains, rising so
abruptly at their backs that one wonders they don't get
toppled over into the water by these protecting giants.
Each of these minor *Dorfen* sends out its wooden jetty, or
its tiny shallop with a flag flying from the stern, to meet the
passing steamers. Ours is one of the slow boats, and we
stop at every such call; others go right on, only stopping
when Coblentz is reached, then again at Bingen and Mayence, or such important places.

But here is Coblentz, where we shall stay over night.
The blue Moselle joins the Rhine's brown waters here.
Truth to tell, the latter liquid is not merely brown, but
decidedly "drumly."   Yonder is the giant rock of Ehren-
breitstein, with its well-kept fortress—a second Gibraltar—
and also recalling Edinburgh Castle to the faithful denizen of
"Auld Reekie."   It is quite a fashionable, busy tourist resort now-a-days, this Coblentz—full of big hotels and noisy
with touters.   But there is the queer old church of St
Castor, and a fine fountain, and the new parade along the
river bank, to take up one's attention while we linger here.
Besides, a good deal of pleasant boating may be done on the
Moselle as well as on the Rhine itself.

Another bright summer morning has just dawned upon us, and here we are breakfasting on the deck of the " Bismarck "— it seems that all the steamers are called after eminent Germans puffing from Coblentz, and rapidly getting to a much more picturesque bit of the river than any we have yet seen. There are sterner hills and more rugged rocks, one of which, with a foaming whirlpool at its feet, is the far-famed Lorlei-berg itself. Alas! the fatal syren who sang there so sweetly to infatuated boatmen has now departed for ever. And no wonder! The East Rhenish Prussia railway has bored a tunnel right through the base of her royal seat, and the shrill shriek of its engines must have proved too much for such a musical ear as hers!

Then yonder are the " Seven Sisters " just popping up their dark heads above water—seven huge blocks of stone, said to be the mortal remains of as many fair maidens who, having offended the river god by refusing various eligible young men favourites of his, it is to be presumed—were thereupon turned into stone—a severe comment on the petrified condition of their hearts previously! Stalwart damsels indeed they appear to have been, and the gap thus created in the family circle must have been no slight one.

But turning from these long past troubles we find ourselves looking with fresh interest on the Pfalz Castle, rearing its white walls from a low rock in mid-stream, then the many towers of Ober-Wezel and the " Golden City " of Bacharach, so called from a supposed resemblance to Jerusalem. There stands the beautiful ruin of St Werner's Church, named after a boy martyr whose body was miraculously floated up the river to this spot.

Another little round fortress rises now from a rocky bed in the river. It is the celebrated " Mause Thurm," or Mouse-tower, where a certain unamiable old bishop was devoured by mice after having refused corn to his starving people, and retired to this wave-guarded castle to enjoy himself in peace. " Amen," says the devout tourist, " so perish all such grasping souls!" And here is Bingen—that "calm Bingen on the Rhine," beloved of all amateur readers and reciters, rather a busy little place it seems to us ; and before long we are in Mayence or Maintz, where our pilgrimage up the river must end. We have been passing through wonderful ranges of vine-fields lately. clothing the hills on each side with their trim green rows and terraces, the Rheingau and Johannisberg being the largest and most famous. And here at Mayence we find a sort of emporium ready to receive the fine vintage of all these, and to disperse it through the world, for it is said there are more than six hundred wine merchants in that tiny city alone! We have just time to run through Mayence and glance at its great cathedral, rich with golden shrines and massive sculptures, before returning to our quiet little retreat down the river, which we had fallen in love with simultaneously, and at once selected for our resting place.—St Goar.

Does anyone want to know of a sweet, quiet village on the Rhine, where he may fare well and cheaply, and enjoy the loveliest scenery, and be within ten minutes' walk of the very finest and largest of the sixty-six ruined castles ? By all means let him go to St Goar. It has the queerest little streets, and the quaintest old KIRCHE, and the sweetest nook of a *Friedhof* imaginable—a very garden of roses which might

half disarm the king of terrors, where the gardener offers you
a bunch of his finest Maréchal Niel, and points to you the
grave of some solitary Englishman, as if he divined at once
what must interest you most. The old saint who gave his
name to the place in the days gone by, is stated to have hung
his cloak on a sunbeam—whether from any deficiency of pegs
in his hermitage or not is left unchronicled—but one can fancy
that something of that gentle power of his that prevailed even
on the flickering sunbeams to wait upon him still lingers about
the place of his dwelling, so attractive did St Goar appear to
our eyes.

And now we are saying good-bye, a long good-bye, to our
queen of rivers. Looking regretfully on the brown waters at
this quiet evening hour as we linger on its banks, we think of
all the old stories and legends they have told us, and once
again as the waves throb and wrestle among the reedy banks,
we seem to hear the plash of long-forgotten oars. Is it the
royal barge of Charlemagne coming slowly up the stream
with floating banners and martial music? or is it Queen
Frastrada, in her coffin of glass, being silently drifted down
towards Aix? or is it the saintly Ursula and her many
maidens? And, yonder on the shore just behind us, may not
that be the hoofs of Roland's palfrey bringing him back from
the Holy Land once more?

The Rhine has all these visitants, and countless others
for every listening ear, from early morning until dewy eve; for
she is a haunted river, and keeps her long train of olden-time
spectres as royally as any olden-time castle with bolts and
bars and rattling chains can do!

One recalls readily by her banks Alexander Smith's fine

poem about the Tweed at Peebles, making one slight altera
tion to suit the name :

> " Who knows? but of this I am certain,
>   That but for the ballads and wails
> That make passionate dead things,—stocks and stones,
>   Make piteous hills and dales ;
> The *Rhine* were as poor as the Amazon,
>   That for all the years it has rolled,
> Can tell but how fair was the morning red,
>   How sweet the evening gold ! "

Robina F. Hardy

IN·NEW·COLLEGE· CHAPEL, OXFORD

MUSIC, on thy wide plumes thou
bear'st me forth
Into the Infinite! My spirit
spurns
Her mortal prison-house, and wildly yearns
Towards the empyrean of her birth :
The starry spaces whence in godlike mirth
The Sons of Morning 'Jubilate' sang,
While from the void abyss Creation sprang.
So this new heaven and diviner earth,
Sprung from thy teeming depths, majestic
Power!
I too would sing! For on thy thunder-tide
Upborne, in rapture of ecstatic pain
From human weakness washed and purified,
I feel a god—with godhood's boundless
dower! . . .
The music dies—and I am dust again.

Noël Paton

Bazaars

THE object of bazaars is threefold :

1. To give persons of moderate income an opportunity of furnishing economically.

2. For the encouragement of Art. At bazaars everything is hand-painted, from cigars to coal-scuttles.

3. To please the men.

WOMAN'S TRUE MISSION.

Most of us must at some time have asked our friends' wives how they could ever have married such men. The reason is that they wanted to marry and settle down to bazaar work.

It does not so much matter whom a woman marries, the great thing is to get into a good bazaar connection.

If women sat in Parliament matters would be quite different. They would buy out the Irish landlords with a bazaar.

The Emin Pasha Relief Committee (says a London correspondent) now regret bitterly that they sent no lady explorers with the Stanley Expedition. It is generally admitted at the clubs that had a lady been left with the Rear Guard she would have inaugurated a bazaar, sold hand-painted rice and tapioca to the natives for fowls, and diddled Tippu Tib out of all his vast possessions.

PREPARING FOR THE BAZAAR.

Among the proudest moments in a man's life is when he exclaims to his wife, " What! another bazaar ?"

He now hurries home every evening from the office, confident that something more has been hand-painted since morning. It may be a table, or vases, or one dozen tobacco pouches, or two fire-screens.

The articles are hand-painted in his private den, because it would be a pity to disarrange the other rooms. He does not object in the least to having to smoke on the door-step.

If he is not doing anything particular would he mind holding up this rocking-chair while she hand-paints it ?

There are twelve young ladies coming to-morrow to hand-paint twelve mantelpiece borders. He will have to see them home.

She writes twenty letters every day to ladies whose addresses she finds in the directory, inviting them to co-operate. This makes many homes happy.

She asks literary characters to write a little thing for the bazaar, because, though she does not know them personally, she is sure they are over-working themselves, and change of work (she has heard) is the best kind of relaxation. They consent with gratitude.

During the three days prior to the bazaar her husband and his friends are allowed to carry the hand-painted articles (which are nearly dry) to cabs. They are also permitted to help in the decking of the stalls. This is great fun.

It never rains on the first day.

The gentleman who opens the bazaar is a prodigious success. He never says that they could have got some one of more eminence than he to discharge these onerous duties, and then waits for cries of " No, no." He always puts things in a way they have never been put before, and when he declares the bazaar open, he never slips away by a side door.

There is no rivalry at the different stalls, for all are working for the cause (see Prospectus).

The articles are sold at great bargains. Nothing is to be raffled, as the committee disapprove of raffling.

Now is your chance for a hand-painted writing desk.

Men enter briskly, as if eager to begin buying at once. There is no hanging back at the doors nor buttoning of coats.

The ladies who serve are anxious that you should buy nothing except what you really want. Are you dying for a hand-painted soup tureen ?

There is still the same desire to let you decide for yourself what you are to buy. Perhaps you have only dropped in to look round ? You are welcome.

None of the articles have been reduced in price, because somehow they did not sell yesterday.

Not one of the ladies serving has wakened with a head-

ache and sent an excuse for her non-appearance. All are as
enthusiastic as ever.

Among the men buying are a great number who were
here yesterday, and have come back because they enjoyed
themselves so much.

No man says that unfortunately he left his purse in his
other coat, nor that he is merely fixing to-day on what he
would like to have that he may come back and buy it
to-morrow.

The hand-painting comes off nothing while in your pocket.

THE LAST DAY.

Ladies do not now arrive in great numbers, because on
the last day things are sold for a mere song.

No contributors are angry because their hand-painted ink
bottles have not sold.

No man is ordered to buy his wife's contributions because
they are still on sale.

No one goes home with dolls in hand-painted pinafores,
and sits on them in the hansom.

There is no desperate raffling of screens at twenty guineas
on the last day.

The committee are still as polite as ever.

The stallholders are quite delighted with the way everything has been managed; and can you tell them of any
minister who wants a new church, hand-painted or plain?

J. M. Barrie

Madrigal

HARK ! the merry wedding bell
  Peals its changing notes of gladness,
    Giving holiday to sadness,
Sweet and low its accents swell.
Loud it tells of hearts united :
Low it breathes of love requited.
Where the mortal who says no,
When sly Cupid bends his bow ?
Thus it comes to one and all,
Be they great or be they small,
Love will chain them in his thrall.
  Sing fal ! lal ! lal !

Fools who rail at Hymen's bliss
Cease your jealous idle scorning !
Taste the dew of love's fresh morning,
Heave soft sigh and steal sweet kiss.
Swift the flower of life is blowing,
Ripening fast for passions glowing ;
Cull its blossom while you may,
Death to-morrow ! Love to-day.
And 'twill come to you as all,
Be they great or be they small,
Love will chain you in his thrall.
  Sing fal ! lal ! lal !

George A. Peacock

The End of It

I GAVE my heart to a woman—
   I gave it her branch and root.
She bruised, she wrung, she tortured,
   She cast it under foot.

Under her feet she cast it,
   She trampled it where it fell.
She broke it all to pieces,
   And each was a clot of hell.

There in the rain and the sunshine,
   They lay and smouldered long :
And each, when again she viewed them,
   Had turned to a living song.

W. E. Henley

TURNBULL AND SPEARS
PRINTERS
EDINBURGH